SNOW DOG, SAND DOG

Linda Joy Singleton

Illustrations by Jess Golden

Albert Whitman & Company
Chicago, Illinois

To Verla Kay, whose photo of a snow dog inspired this book.
Also to my supportive parents, Ed and Nina, and wonderful husband, David —L.J.S.

For my cheerleaders, Mom & Dad —J.G.

Library of Congress Cataloging-in-Publication data is on file with the publisher.

Text copyright © 2014 by Linda Joy Singleton
Illustrations copyright © 2014 by Albert Whitman & Company
Published in 2014 by Albert Whitman & Company
ISBN 978-0-8075-7536-9

Printed in China.
10 9 8 7 6 5 4 3 2 1 NP 18 17 16 15 14 13

The design is by Nick Tiemersma.

For more information about Albert Whitman & Company,
visit our web site at www.albertwhitman.com.

More than anything, Ally wanted a dog.

But dogs made her ACHOO!

So Ally drew pictures of dogs.
Fancy dogs, scruffy dogs, wrinkly dogs, and curly dogs.
But Ally couldn't draw the one she really wanted.
A real dog of her own.

When it snowed, Ally ran outside to play.
Other kids were making snowmen.

Ally made a snow dog.

She gave him pebble eyes, a pinecone collar, and a crooked icicle tail.

The other kids laughed and said,
"There's no such thing as a snow dog."

"Yes, there is," Ally said.

And when Ally left, Snow Dog followed her home.

He sat by the freezer
instead of the fire.

They slurped Popsicles and
played fetch with snowballs.

They napped in igloos

then made dog angels in the snow.

But when the spring sun came,
the snow melted...

And so did Snow Dog.

Ally stared out the window watching
puppies play and wished for snow.

When spring blossomed, Ally went outside to play.
Other kids were picking flowers for bouquets.

Ally made a flower dog.

She gave him seedpod eyes,
a daisy-chain collar, and a crooked stick tail.

The other kids laughed and said,
"There's no such thing as a flower dog."

"Yes, there is," Ally said.

And when Ally left, Flower Dog followed her home.

He plopped on a planter
instead of a rug.

They chased butterflies
and played fetch with
garden gnomes.

They napped in a flower bed

then floated petal boats in a stream.

But when the summer sky blazed,
flowers withered away...

And so did Flower Dog.

When it was time for summer vacation,
Ally's parents took her to the beach.

Ally waded in the ocean and watched a puppy chase a Frisbee. She tossed sticks into the waves then waited for them to return. Other kids built sand castles. Ally built a sand dog.

She gave him sand dollar eyes, a seaweed collar, and a crooked driftwood tail.

The other kids laughed and said,
"There's no such thing as a sand dog."

"Yes, there is," Ally said.

And when Ally left,
Sand Dog followed her home.

He curled up in the sandbox instead of a doggy bed.

They chewed saltwater taffy and played fetch with seashells.

They napped on beach towels then dug for treasure in the sandbox.

But when fall winds gusted,
dry sand drifted away...

And so did Sand Dog.

When autumn leaves piled higher
than cars, Ally took a rake outside.

Other kids were jumping in leaf hills.
Ally made a leaf dog.

She gave him acorn eyes,
a cranberry collar,
and a crooked twig tail.

The other kids laughed and said,
"There's no such thing as a leaf dog."

"Yes, there is," Ally said.

And when Ally left,
Leaf Dog followed her home.

He perched on a pumpkin
instead of a pillow.

They heated popcorn and
played fetch with straw brooms.

They napped with a scarecrow then danced
to the music of wind chimes.

But when winter winds gusted, brittle leaves tumbled away...
And so did Leaf Dog.

Ally went inside and took out her sketch pad.

She drew pictures of dogs with button eyes, flowery seaweed collars, and crooked stick tails.

One day Ally woke up and shivered with cold. She looked out her window. The sky was winter white, trees sparkled with crystal ice, and big snowflakes drifted to the ground.

Laughing, Ally jumped out of bed. She put on her jacket, hat, and mittens.

Then she raced outside
to sled with Snow Dog.

In the spring she floated
petals with Flower Dog.

In the summer she fetched
seashells with Sand Dog.

In the fall she heated
popcorn with Leaf Dog.

And none of her dogs made her
ACHOO.

How to Make a Dog without Snow

Just because you don't have snow doesn't mean you can't have a snow dog! Here's how to make one with things you can find around your house.

Materials

- Three empty cardboard toilet paper rolls for legs and neck
- Small box for body (no bigger than a shoe box)
- Small milk carton for head (such as the kind you get from a school lunch)
- Cardboard for paws (an empty cereal box works great)
- Cotton balls
- Scissors
- Glue
- Heavy duty tape (like duct tape) to attach tricky parts
- For eyes, ears, tail, tongue, and other decorations, try to collect some of these objects: buttons, coins, colored paper, felt, acorns, seeds, tape, pipe cleaners, beads, glitter, aluminum foil, paint, sticks, sequins, bottle lids, string, or anything else you can find! Get creative!

Directions

1. Cut two of the toilet paper rolls in half to create four dog legs.

2. Cut the third cardboard tube to the length you want for the dog's neck. Use glue to connect the tube to the box-body and the milk-carton-head. We recommend keeping the milk carton on its side with the spout toward the front—if you keep the spout open, it makes a great mouth.) Use tape to secure parts if needed. Don't worry too much about being neat since you'll cover up the body with the cotton ball fur.

3. Glue four toilet paper-roll legs beneath the dog body. You can use tape to secure if needed.

4. Cut cardboard to make paws and glue to the bottom of the legs.

5. Tear and stretch the cotton balls and glue them all over your snow dog for fur.

6. Use the rest of the objects you gathered to decorate your snow dog!

How creative can you be?

Visit www.lindajoysingleton.com or www.albertwhitman.com to find pictures of this project and much more.